For Hunter
—A.I.

To Rebecca, for always
reminding me that I'm not little
—G.T.

 little bee books

An imprint of Bonnier Publishing USA
251 Park Avenue South, New York, NY 10010
Text copyright © 2017 by Alison Inches
Illustrations copyright © 2017 by Bonnier Publishing USA
All rights reserved, including the right of reproduction
in whole or in part in any form. LITTLE BEE BOOKS is a trademark
of Bonnier Publishing USA, and associated colophon
is a trademark of Bonnier Publishing USA.
ISBN 9781499803778 (hardcover) | LCCN 2016001017
Manufactured in China   LEO 1216
First Edition
2 4 6 8 10 9 7 5 3 1
Library of Congress Cataloging-in-Publication Data
Names: Inches, Alison, author. | Thomas, Glenn, illustrator.
Title: I'm not little! / by Alison Inches; illustrated by Glenn Thomas.
Other titles: I am not little
Description: First edition. | New York, New York: Little Bee Books, [2017]
Summary: Little Shaggy, a fuzzy little monster, is tired of everyone
calling him little until his mother brings his new baby sister home and
Little Shaggy suddenly misses being the youngest.
Subjects: | CYAC: Size—Fiction. | Monsters—Fiction.
Classification: LCC PZ7.I355 Im 2017 | DDC [E]—dc23
LC record available at https://lccn.loc.gov/2016001017

littlebeebooks.com
bonnierpublishingusa.com

I'M NOT LITTLE!

by
Alison Inches

illustrated by
Glenn Thomas

little bee books

Little Shaggy has a
fuzzy little coat,
skinny little arms...

and sharp little teeth.

Papa calls him
Little Buddy.

Mama calls him Little Love Bug—
and sometimes Little Fussbudget.

Fur Pa calls him
Little Whippersnapper.

Fur Ma says,
"Is that your little car?"

All day long
they say,

"Here's your fuzzy little blanket!"

"Would you like a little snack?"

"Where's your little chew toy?"

"How about a little story?"

"Let's go for a little walk!"

"Are you a little grumpy?"

"What a cute little fluff ball!"

But you know what?

Little Shaggy has a little news.

Then Little Shaggy has
a little temper tantrum.

He jumps on his bed and
makes a mess at breakfast.

He throws his
little farm animals.

He pulls his fur and
stomps his little feet.

Little clumps of monster fluff
scatter across the floor.

"I do not want
my little blanket
or a little snack!"

"No more
little walks
or little
fluff ball
talk!"

"And you know what?
My name is SHAGGY!

Not **LITTLE** Shaggy.

And my little chew toy
is a little LOST!"

Then Mama taps Shaggy
on the shoulder.

"May I say one more LITTLE thing?" she asks.

"I want you to meet your
brand-new little sister!"

"My brand-new little **what**?"

"Your little baby sister!"

"You are now a great BIG brother!"

"...But I DON'T WANT TO BE BIG!"

"That's okay...."

"You will always be Mama's Little Angel."

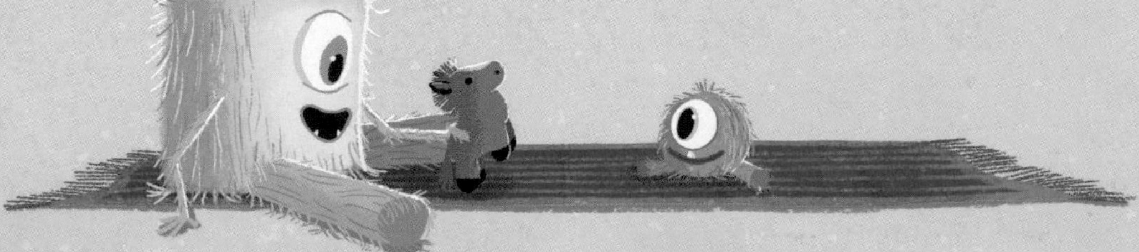